Waiting-for-Spring Stories

Waiting-for-Spring Stories

E
C.3

by Bethany Roberts

illustrations by
William Joyce

Harper & Row, Publishers

Library of Congress Cataloging in Publication Data
Roberts, Bethany.
    Waiting-for-spring stories.

    Summary: As the family passes the winter in their
cozy home, Papa Rabbit tells them stories about other
rabbits.
    [1. Rabbits—Fiction]   I. Joyce, William, ill.
II. Title.
PZ7.R5396Wai 1984   [E]   83-49486
ISBN 0-06-025061-5
ISBN 0-06-025062-3 (lib. bdg.)

Designed by Constance Fogler
1 2 3 4 5 6 7 8 9 10
First Edition

To Krista and Melissa,
who clamor for "homemade stories"

B. R.

To the kindest, most generous man I know—
my father

W. J.

As winter snows fall gently on rabbit homes, all rabbit families pass the long time until spring by telling tales.

And so, in this cozy house, Papa Rabbit, like Grandpa Rabbit before him, and Great-Grandpa Rabbit before that, is getting ready to tell waiting-for-spring stories to his family.

Listen as Papa puts another log on the fire and begins.

The Wind
and the Clothes

Once an old rabbit was hanging his clothes on a line. The wind came along and blew them off.

Whoosh! Off went a sock.

Whoosh! Off went a shirt.

Whoosh! Off went a jacket and a bathrobe and a pair of pants.

"Give me back my clothes!" cried the rabbit.

"Finders keepers, losers weepers," said the wind.

The rabbit ran to catch his clothes. But the wind blew them into a tree.

"Why do you want my clothes?" asked the rabbit.

"I am cold," said the wind.

"My clothes are too small for you," said the rabbit.

"So they are," said the wind with a sigh.

"Give me back my clothes, and I will tell you what to do," said the rabbit.

The wind blew the clothes down from the tree. They fell on the ground.

"Now tell me what to do," the wind demanded.

"There is a long, woolly cloud," said the rabbit. "Use it for a scarf."

The wind put on the scarf-cloud.

"Absolutely splendid," said the wind.

"And there is a small, puffy cloud," said the rabbit. "Use that for a hat."

The wind put on the hat-cloud.

"Gloriously grand," said the wind.

"And there are two short, fleecy clouds," said the rabbit. "Use them for mittens."

The wind put on the mitten-clouds.

"Positively perfect," said the wind.

"Now are you warm, Wind?" asked the rabbit.

"Yes, thank you, Rabbit," said the wind.

So the rabbit hung up his clothes again and went inside.

The Dark Forest

A rabbit took a walk in a dark forest. Soon he heard a noise.

Thump, thump! went the noise.

The rabbit walked a little faster.

Thumpity-thump! went the noise. It was moving faster, too.

The rabbit began to run. He ran and ran. The noise thumped behind him. The faster the rabbit ran, the faster the noise thumped.

Just ahead, the rabbit saw the end of the woods.

"If I can get to the end of the woods, I think I will be safe," said the rabbit.

The rabbit ran as hard as he could. The noise thumped right behind him.

At last the rabbit came to the end of the woods. He flopped down under a nearby tree.

"Oh," he sighed, "I cannot run another step. I will have to wait here and see what happens."

"Oh," said a voice. The voice huffed and puffed. "I am so glad you stopped. I was getting very tired."

"Who are you?" cried the rabbit. He looked into the woods.

Out of the woods came the rabbit's shadow.

"A dark forest is no place for a shadow," said the shadow. It flopped down next to the rabbit.

The rabbit and his shadow rested together. Then they walked home in the sunshine.

The Wishing Star

One night a rabbit made a wish on a star.

"I wish I could be a sea captain," said the rabbit.

"Forget it," said the star.

"But you are a wishing star," said the rabbit.
"You have to give me my wish."

"Why should I give you a wish?" asked the star.
"Nobody ever gives me a wish."

"What do you wish?" asked the rabbit.

"I wish I could sing," said the star.

"Maybe you need music," said the rabbit. He ran home to get a flute. He played the flute for the star.

The star opened its mouth. But nothing came out.

"No," said the star, "that does not help me sing."

"Maybe you need dancing," said the rabbit. The rabbit danced around and around.

The star tried to sing again.

"It's no use," said the star. "I still cannot sing."

"Maybe you need someone to sing to," said the rabbit. "There is a sleepy little star. Sing to it."

The star sang to the little star. It sang the little star to sleep.

"I can sing!" shouted the star.

"There is your wish," said the rabbit.

"And here is yours," sang the star, as the rabbit sailed away at the wheel of his ship.

The Spring Shower

Once two little rabbits got caught in a spring shower. They looked for a dry spot to rest until the shower ended. They found a hole in the ground. But their ears stuck out.

"Too small," said one.

"Too small," agreed the other.

They found a place under a bush. But their feet stuck out.

"Too small," said one.

"Too small," agreed the other.

They found a hollow in a tree. But their tails stuck out.

"Too small," said one.

"Too small," agreed the other.

They could not find a spot big enough for both of them at once.

"I know," said the first rabbit, "I will keep you dry." He held his coat over his friend's head. His ears got wet. His paws got wet. His tail got wet.

"Now it is my turn," said the second rabbit. "I will keep *you* dry." He held the coat over his friend's head. His whiskers got wet. His nose got wet. His back got wet.

Then the rain stopped. The sun came out, and the two little rabbits went home. They found a dry towel. They each tried to wrap up in it.

"Too big," said one.

"Too big," agreed the other.

So they sat, side by side, together in the warm towel.

"Just right," said one.

"Just right for two," agreed his friend.

The Garden

Once a farmer rabbit was working in his garden. He pulled up an onion.

"Ouch!" said the onion.

He pulled up a carrot.

"Ouch!" said the carrot.

He pulled up a potato.

"Ouch!" said the potato.

"Stop that!" said the farmer rabbit. "You have to come up and be my dinner."

The farmer took the onion, the carrot, and the potato into the kitchen.

"If you cut me, I will make you cry," said the onion.

"That is silly," said the farmer rabbit. He cut into the onion. Soon large tears ran down his cheeks.

"I can't see!" he cried.

"Get him, boys," called the onion.

The potato rolled off the table. The farmer tripped over the potato, dropped the onion, and fell.

"Ow, my leg!" he cried.

The carrot rolled off the table. It whacked the farmer on the head.

"Ouch, my head!" he wailed.

"This way, boys," called the onion.

The carrot, the potato, and the onion all rolled out the door.

"I have had enough," said the farmer. "I will never eat onions, or carrots, or potatoes again."

After that, the farmer rabbit always ate pancakes for his dinner.

The Little Rabbit
with Big Feet

Once there was a little rabbit with big feet. His feet were not very happy.

The little rabbit tried to run. But he bumped into trees and bushes.

"Ouch!" said the little rabbit's feet. "Be careful!"

The little rabbit tried to skip. But he tripped over rocks and roots.

"Look where you are going!" said the little rabbit's feet.

The little rabbit tried to dance. But he walked on the feet of all the other rabbit dancers.

"Watch your step!" cried the other rabbits. The little rabbit's feet just moaned.

The little rabbit tried to shrink his feet. He put them into a tub of water. He sat and sat.

"You are making us wrinkled," said his feet. And they did not get any smaller.

The little rabbit tried to shorten his feet. He put them into tiny shoes. He squeezed and squeezed.

"That hurts!" said his feet. And it did not make them any smaller, either.

"A little rabbit needs little feet. But a big rabbit needs big feet. Have a carrot," said the little rabbit's feet.

Time came. Time went. The little rabbit's ears grew. His arms grew. His legs grew. Soon he was the biggest rabbit in the woods. And his feet were exactly the right size for the rest of him.

"Now, that's better," said his feet. "We never knew a problem that a carrot couldn't solve."

The Hunt for Spring

Once a little rabbit was waiting for spring.

"I have not seen Spring yet," she thought. "Spring must be lost."

"Spring!" called the little rabbit. "Do not worry. I am coming to find you."

The little rabbit ran through the woods.

"Yoo-hoo!" she called. "Spring, are you here?"

"That rabbit is noisy," complained the robins.

The little rabbit ran through the meadow.

"Spring," she cried, "where are you?"

"What a loud rabbit," said the flowers.

The little rabbit ran by the stream.

"Hello!" she yelled. "Can you hear me, Spring?"

"What is all the noise about?" asked the grass.

"Spring must be lost forever. Boo-hoo!" sobbed the little rabbit. She sat down to cry.

"Watch it!" said a worm. "You almost sat on me."

"Sorry," sniffed the little rabbit, "but I am sad. Spring is lost."

"Lost? Try twitching your nose," said the worm.

The little rabbit twitched her nose.

"Um-m," she said. "Flowers."

"Now, wiggle your ears," said the worm.

The little rabbit wiggled her ears.

"Oh!" said the little rabbit. "Birds!"

"And now," said the worm, "look at your feet."

The little rabbit looked down at her feet.

"My," said the little rabbit. "Fresh, green grass."

"Flowers, birds, and grass," said the worm. "Now, how do you feel?"

"Springy!" cried the little rabbit as she kicked up her heels and skipped away.

When bright sunlight pours into rabbit homes, and the snow begins to melt from the windowpanes, storytelling comes to an end.

Papa Rabbit, like Grandpa Rabbit before him, and Great-Grandpa Rabbit before that, has told enough waiting-for-spring stories. For his little rabbit children, there will be no more waiting.

Spring is here at last!